DATE DUE

DEMCO 38-296

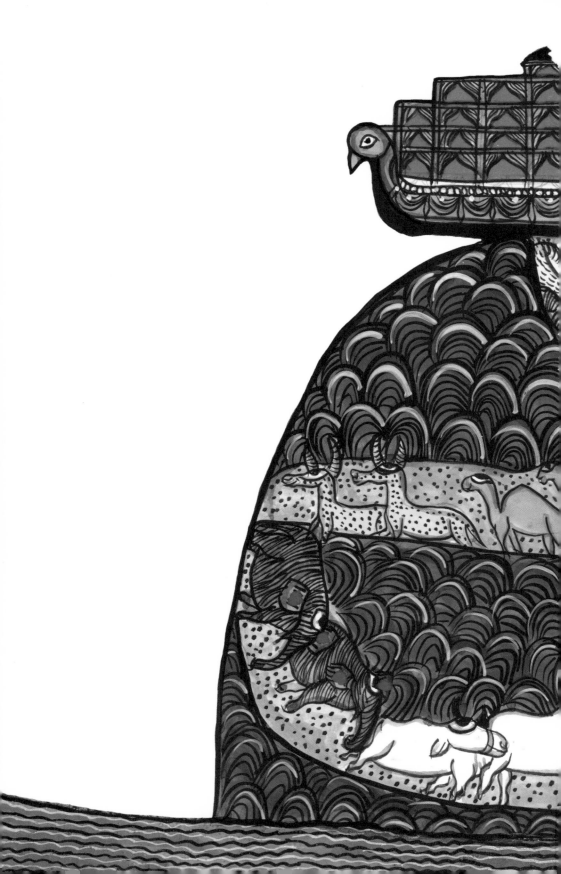

They say that from time to time, the world must be made all over again. Ancient stories remember an age when a huge flood destroyed the earth. Almost everything as we know it disappeared under water, and it was only later, in the course of time, that new life emerged again from remains of the old. You may have heard this story before, but great tales deserve to be repeated – and so let me tell it here again, in my way.

Noah was resolute, and sent out a dove on the same mission. But the dove was unsuccessful as well. Noah did not give up, but waited, and after seven days, sent the dove out again. This time she returned bearing a fresh olive branch. It was an offering of peace, a sign of trust from God. Noah felt encouraged, and sent the dove out a third time – and this time she stayed away. She had found a place to land.

Following this good omen, Noah and Na'mah felt bold enough to leave the ark and come down the mountain, with all the animals in their keeping.

The ground was marshy and difficult, but they toiled on through the bog, until one day they spotted dry land. Here they rested after their ordeal, thankful for finding land that could sustain them all.

When God first created the world, he was satisfied. Land, sea, and sky, with all their creatures, lived together in harmony.

But as time passed, he saw a change come over human beings. No longer content, they wanted more and more. Without a sense of their real needs, and fed by greed, they began to attack each other and plunder the earth. God was shaken. To caution the human race and teach them a lesson, he decided to wipe away the world that was turning so ugly, and create a better one in its place.

God looked for a steadfast person to carry out his plans, a human being who would endure all the travails that were to come, and pass on the wisdom he earned to coming generations. He chose a mindful man called Noah.

One night, God came to Noah and his wife Na'mah in a dream, telling them that a great flood would submerge the earth and swallow all life. But Noah and Na'mah would be saved, if they heeded his plan, and carried it out with care.

God told them to first build a big, strong ark, a safe haven to see them through the flood.

I nside the ark, Na'mah tended each animal on board, and Noah prayed for all their safety. On the forty first day, a small wind began to blow, growing stronger and harder, until it pushed the rain back into the sky.

The waters started to recede gradually, until the tip of a mountain appeared on the horizon. The ark drifted over to it.

Berthed on top of the mountain, the castaways looked about with hope. But they could see no ground where they could step out.

So Noah sent out a raven to scout for dry ground. The bird soared in all four directions, but finding no place to land, returned to the ark.

Then they were to go out and look for a pair – a male and a female – of every sort of animal they could find on land, water and air. After the flood had swept away all other living things, these creatures would create new life.

Once the ark was ready, Noah and Na'mah set out on their search.

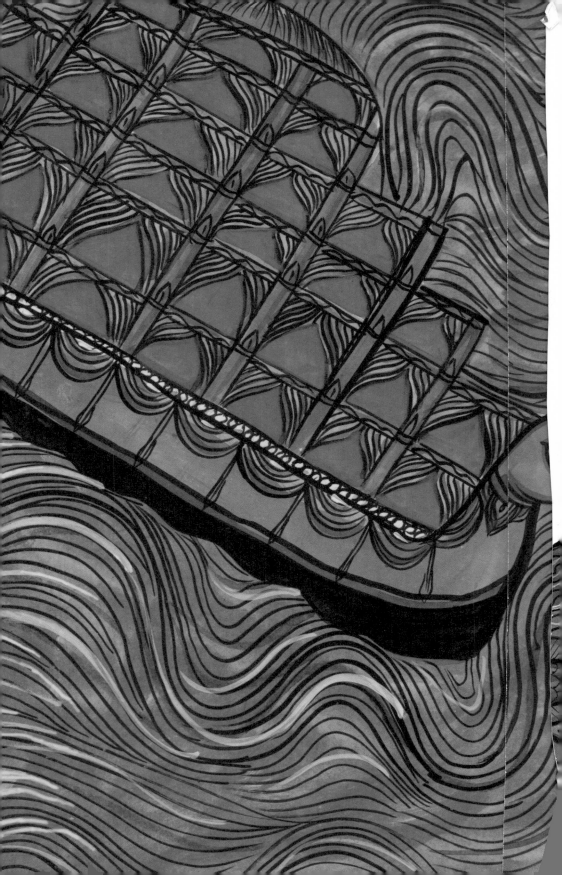

The only thing on the horizon was the tiny ark, tossed around by tall waves. But it held fast, shielding all the creatures in its safekeeping.

It rained without a break, for forty days and nights. The flood waters swept away every living thing: trees, people, animals and birds.

Slowly, the ground sank under the rising water like a huge stone, until nothing, not even the top of the highest mountain, was visible.

They found all forms of creatures: large and small, fierce and tame, with feet, and fins, wearing fur, scales and feathers.

At last, satisfied with their gathering, Noah and Na'mah returned to the ark, followed by pairs of creatures they had chosen.

Noah herded them in, two by two, and Na'mah gave each pair a place to settle. Then the door of the great ship was closed.

Instantly, the sun vanished and the sky turned black. Rain began to pour like a great waterfall from the sky.